Once upon a time, there lived a lovely little princess named Snow White. Her vain and wicked stepmother, the Queen, feared that one day Snow White's beauty would surpass her own. So she dressed the little princess in rags and forced her to work as a servant in the castle.

Each day, the Queen consulted her magic mirror. 'Magic Mirror on the wall, who is the fairest one of all?' As long as the mirror responded in the Queen's favour, Snow White was safe.

One day, as Snow White was drawing water from a well, she made a wish. She wished that the one she loved would find her, and she dreamed about how nice he would be. As she gazed into the wishing well, she saw another face reflected in the water. It belonged to a handsome prince!

'Hello. Did I frighten you? Please don't run away!'

But the startled princess had fled to her balcony where she could watch him from afar.

This is the story of Snow White.
You can read along with me in your
book. You will know it is time to turn
the page when you hear the chimes
ring like this...

Let's begin now:

Narrator	Mary D'Arcy
The Queen	Eda Reiss Merin
The Prince	Jerry Whitman
Magic Mirror	Tony Jay
The Huntsman	Peter Renaday
Snow White	Mary Kay Bergman
Doc	Hal Smith
Grumpy	Corey Burton

Produced by Randy Thornton and Ted Kryczko
Adapted by Randy Thornton
Engineered by George Charouhas

Heigh-Ho
Performed by the Dwarf Chorus
Music by Frank Churchill
Lyrics by Larry Morey
© 1938 Bourne Co. (ASCAP). © renewed. All rights reserved.
International © secured. Used by permission.
℗ 2003 Walt Disney Records

This edition published by Parragon in 2012

Parragon
Queen Street House
4 Queen Street
Bath BA1 1HE, UK
www.parragon.com

ISBN 978-1-4454-8358-0

Printed in China

At that moment, the Queen was spying on Snow White and the Prince. When she saw them together, she flew into a jealous rage and rushed to her Magic Mirror, demanding an answer.

'Famed is thy beauty, Majesty, but hold! A lovely maid I see. Rags cannot hide her gentle grace. She is more fair than thee.'

'Alas for her! Reveal her name.'

'Lips red as a rose, hair black as ebony, skin white as snow...'
'SNOW WHITE!'

Furious, the Queen sent for her Huntsman. 'Take Snow White far into the forest. Find some secluded glade where she can pick wildflowers. And there, my faithful Huntsman, you will kill her!'

'But Your Majesty – the little princess!'

'Silence! You know the penalty if you fail.'

Knowing that he dare not disobey the Queen, the Huntsman led Snow White into the forest. But when it came time for him to harm Snow White, he stopped and fell to his knees.

'I can't do it. Forgive me, Your Highness!'

'Why, why – I don't understand!'

'The Queen is mad! She's jealous of you. She'll stop at nothing. Now quick, child – run, run away. Hide in the woods. Anywhere! And never come back!'

Frightened and alone, Snow White ran into the forest. Blazing eyes peered out at her from the darkness. Eerie shrieks pierced the air. The branches of trees grabbed at her. Finally she could run no farther, and collapsed to the ground, sobbing.

When Snow White looked up, she saw several forest animals gathered around her. 'Hello. Do you know where I can stay? Maybe in the woods somewhere?'

Snow White followed the animals to a charming little cottage in the woods. She knocked on the door, but no-one answered. So she went inside.

'Oh, it's adorable! Just like a doll's house. What a cute little chair. Why, there's seven little chairs. There must be seven little children. And by the looks of this table, seven untidy children. I know, I'll clean house and surprise them, then maybe they'll let me stay.'

With the help of her animal friends, Snow White cleaned the cottage in no time. Then she decided to check upstairs. 'What adorable little beds. And look, they have names carved on them: Doc, Happy, Sneezy, Dopey ... what funny names for children! And there's Grumpy, Bashful and Sleepy. I'm a little sleepy myself.' Snow White lay down across three of the tiny beds and fell asleep.

Just then, the owners of the cottage came marching home. They weren't children at all, but Seven Dwarfs who worked all day in their diamond mine.

Snow White pleaded with her hosts. 'Please don't send me away! If you do, the Queen will kill me!'

Grumpy shook his head. 'The Queen's an old witch. If she finds you here, she'll swoop down and wreak her vengeance on all of us!'

'Oh, she'll never find me here. And if you let me stay, I'll keep house for you. I'll wash and sew and sweep and cook ...'

'Cook!' Doc rubbed his tummy. 'Hooray! She stays!'

Doc dashed behind the beds, and the other Dwarfs ran after him.

Snow White yawned and stretched. Then she noticed seven pairs of eyes looking at her over the end of the beds. She sat up, smiling. 'How do you do?'

'How do you do what?' Grumpy folded his arms, scowling.

Snow White laughed. 'Let me guess. You must be Grumpy.'

'Heh! I know who I am. Who are you?'

'Oh, how silly of me. I'm Snow White.'

'The princess?' Doc looked very impressed, but Grumpy frowned. 'Tell her to go back to where she belongs.'

Suddenly, the Dwarfs thought they heard a sound. Doc looked toward the stairs. 'I-i-it's up there. In the bedroom.'

Cautiously, the seven little men went to investigate. Doc slowly opened the door and peered in. 'Why, i-i-it's a girl!'

As the Dwarfs approached the sleeping princess, she began to stir.

'She's wakin' up! Hide!'

As they came into the clearing, the one named Doc made everyone halt. He peered through his glasses.

'Look – our house! The lit's light! Uh ... the light's lit! Door's open. Chimney's smokin'. Somethin's in there!'

The Dwarfs peeked inside the cottage. Doc gasped. 'Why, why, the whole place is clean!'

Grumpy, true to his name, crossed his arms and glared. 'Mark my words, there's trouble a-brewin'. I felt it comin' on all day.'

Back in the castle, the wicked Queen stood before her mirror. 'Magic Mirror on the wall, who now is the fairest one of all?'

'Beyond the seventh fall, in the cottage of the Seven Dwarfs, Snow White still lives, fairest one of all.'

'I've been tricked! I'll go myself, to the Dwarfs' cottage in the woods. I'll go in a disguise so complete, no-one will suspect me.'

The Queen concocted a magic potion, then transformed herself into an ugly old peddler woman 'And now, a special sort of death for one so fair. What should it be? Ah, a poisoned apple! One taste, and Snow White's eyes will close forever, only to be revived by Love's First Kiss. No fear of that! The Dwarfs will think she's dead!'

  Back at the cottage, Snow White was saying goodbye to the Dwarfs as they set off for work. As she kissed each one on the head, Doc stood close by. 'Now don't forget, my dear, the old Queen's a sly one. Full of witchcraft, so beware.'

  Then Grumpy frowned. 'Now, I'm warnin' ya – don't let nobody or nothin' in the house!'

  Snow White smiled at him. 'Why, Grumpy, you do care!'

  'Heh.'

Shortly after the Dwarfs left, the old peddler woman appeared at the cottage. 'All alone, my pet?'

Snow White nodded as the old woman sniffed the air. 'Makin' pies?'

'Yes, gooseberry pies.'

'Ah, it's apple pies that make the menfolks' mouths water. Pies made with apples like these.' She lifted a shiny red apple from her basket.

'Like to try one, dearie, hmmm? Go on, have a bite.'

Sensing that Snow White was in danger, several birds swooped down on the woman, knocking the apple out of her hand.

Snow White tried to shoo the birds away. 'Stop it! Go away! Shame on you, frightening the poor old lady.'

'Oh, my heart. Oh, my. My poor heart. Take me into the house, and let me rest. A drink of water, please.'

Unable to make Snow White understand, the birds and animals raced to alert the Dwarfs. At the mine, they pulled and tugged at the confused little men. Grumpy growled. 'What ails these crazy critters? They ain't actin' this way for nothin'.'

Doc thought about it. 'Maybe it's – the Queen!'

Grumpy galloped off on the back of a deer. 'Snow White's in danger! We've gotta save her!'

Meanwhile, the Queen picked up the poisoned apple. 'Because you've been so good to poor old granny, I'll share a secret with you. This is no ordinary apple. It's a magic wishing apple!'

'A wishing apple? Really?'

'Yes. One bite and all your dreams will come true.'

The old woman grinned at the princess. 'Perhaps there's someone you love.'

Snow White remembered her prince. 'Well, there is someone.'

'I thought so. Old Granny knows a young girl's heart. Now make a wish and take a bite.'

Snow White did so. 'Oh, I feel strange.' A moment later, she fell to the ground.

 A sudden storm began to rage as the Dwarfs reached the cottage, where they found the lifeless Snow White. Through the rain, Grumpy spotted the old hag disappearing into the forest. 'There she goes, men! After her!'
 The Dwarfs chased the Queen up a steep cliff. 'You little fools, I'll crush your bones!' She tried desperately to pry a boulder loose to crush them. Suddenly, a bolt of lightning shattered the ledge, sending the wicked Queen into the valley below.

Though the evil Queen was gone forever, the princess was still locked in her spell. So beautiful was she, even in death, the Dwarfs could not find it in their hearts to bury her.

Doc brushed away a tear. 'Let's make her a coffin out of glass and gold. That way, we can still see her and keep constant watch by her side.'

The Prince heard of the beautiful maiden who slept in the glass coffin. He rode to the cottage of the Seven Dwarfs, and they took him to Snow White. Gently, he kissed her. Then, slowly, her eyes began to open. The spell was broken. Love's First Kiss had brought her back to life!

Snow White's wish finally came true. She bid the Seven Dwarfs goodbye as the handsome prince swept her into his arms. Soon wedding bells rang, echoing throughout the forest. From then on, Snow White and her Prince Charming lived in their castle in the clouds ... happily ever after.

The End